Miffy
Jumps for Joy

Based on the work of **Dick Bruna**
Story written by **Natalie Shaw**

SIMON SPOTLIGHT

New York London Toronto Sydney New Delhi

SIMON SPOTLIGHT
An imprint of Simon & Schuster Children's Publishing Division
1230 Avenue of the Americas, New York, New York 10020
This Simon Spotlight paperback edition May 2017
Published in 2017 by Simon & Schuster, Inc.
Publication licensed by Mercis Publishing bv, Amsterdam.
Stories and images are based on the work of Dick Bruna.
'Miffy and Friends' © copyright Mercis Media bv, all rights reserved.
All rights reserved, including the right of reproduction in whole or in part in any form.
SIMON SPOTLIGHT and colophon are registered trademarks of Simon & Schuster, Inc.
For information about special discounts for bulk purchases, please contact Simon & Schuster Special Sales
at 1-866-506-1949 or business@simonandschuster.com.
Manufactured in the United States of America 0317 LAK
2 4 6 8 10 9 7 5 3 1
ISBN 978-1-4814-9172-3 (pbk)
ISBN 978-1-4814-9173-0 (eBook)

Miffy is in a hurry to get home! She is running.
"Today was the last day of school, and Daddy says he
has a surprise for me and my friends!" says Miffy.

Miffy sees Daddy working hard to pump air into a bouncy castle!

"Wow, a bouncy castle! What a lovely surprise!" says Miffy. "Thank you, Daddy!"

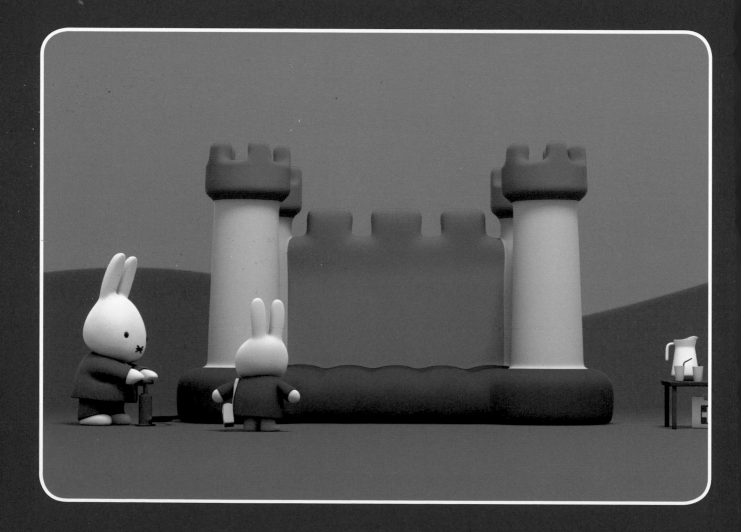

"I can't wait to show you how it works!" Daddy says.
But before he can, Miffy hops onto the bouncy castle all by herself.
"I'll let you go first, then," Daddy says.

"It's hard to walk on it. It's so springy!" Miffy says as she tries it out. Then Miffy falls on her bottom and adds, "But it doesn't hurt if you fall over!"

Next Miffy falls over on purpose . . . and bounces right back up again!
"Wahoo!" she says.

Miffy bounces up and down.
"That's it, Miffy!" Daddy tells her.
"This is great!" Miffy shouts.
"It is a boingy one, isn't it?" Daddy says to himself.
He can't wait to try it out!

Miffy stops for a drink. That's when Melanie comes by!
"Oh wow!" Melanie says, looking at the bouncy castle.
"Hi, Melanie!" Miffy says. "Ready for a bounce?"
"Yeah!" Melanie cries.

They don't realize that Daddy was about to try the bouncy castle.

Maybe I'll go in a minute, Daddy thinks.

Miffy and Melanie climb on and start bouncing.

"One, two, three, and bottom bounce!" Miffy says, and she and Melanie bounce on their bottoms!

"Watch this, Daddy!" Miffy says. "One, two, three!"
Miffy and Melanie jump at the same time!
"Oh yes, that looks like great fun!" Daddy says. "What if we try it with *three* bouncing?"
"That is a good idea!" says Miffy.

That is when Grunty arrives.

"Make room for Grunty," she says. Then she notices the first aid kit. "Why do you have a first aid kit?" Grunty asks Daddy.

"Just in case anyone takes a tumble," Daddy says.

"Don't worry, Grunty, it doesn't hurt even if you do fall over!" says Miffy. "Come on!"
Together, they help Grunty climb onto the bouncy castle and start to bounce!

While they jump, Miffy, Melanie, and Grunty sing a song!

Boing-boing, boing-boing,
jumping really high.
Boing-boing, boing-boing,
reaching to the sky!

While they're jumping, Daddy wonders if they are thirsty.

"Why don't you come down and get a nice cold drink?" he asks.

"No thanks, Daddy," says Miffy.

"Are you sure? Because this lemonade is so cool and refreshing," Daddy says, and takes a sip.

"Maybe just a quick one," says Grunty, and Miffy
and Melanie soon follow.
  The lemonade is delicious!

While they are drinking lemonade, the bouncy castle is empty. Daddy hops on.
"It's a shame to see the castle go to waste," Daddy says to himself. He starts bouncing. "Wahoo!" he says. It is so much fun!

But when Daddy lands on his bottom, he doesn't bounce right back up again. Instead, the bouncy castle makes a popping sound and there is a whoosh of air.

Daddy begins to sink . . . and so does the *whole* bouncy castle.

"Oh no! I've put a hole in it," Daddy says.

Grunty comes running over with the first aid kit.
"Are you okay? Do you need a bandage?" Grunty asks.
"I'm all right, Grunty, thank you," says Daddy.

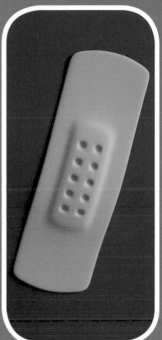

But Miffy has an idea. "A bandage might be useful after all!" she says. "We just have to find the hole!"

Melanie hears a hissing sound. It is the sound of air coming out of the bouncy castle.

"Here it is!" says Melanie, pointing out the hole.

Miffy sticks the bandage over the hole and the hissing sound stops.

Next they need to pump air back into the bouncy castle!

"Here's the pump!" Grunty says.

"And here's the pump power!" Daddy says, meaning himself.

Everyone cheers as Daddy pumps up the bouncy castle. It is hard work!
"Nearly there," Daddy says, panting.

Finally the bouncy castle is ready to go again!

"Thanks, Daddy!" Miffy says. "You can have the first bounce, if you like!"

But Daddy is too tired. Instead, he leans on the bouncy castle . . . and looks very comfortable!

"Maybe we'll just let him have a little rest," Miffy whispers to her friends.

After all, they have had so much fun on the bouncy castle today, and it was all because of Daddy!

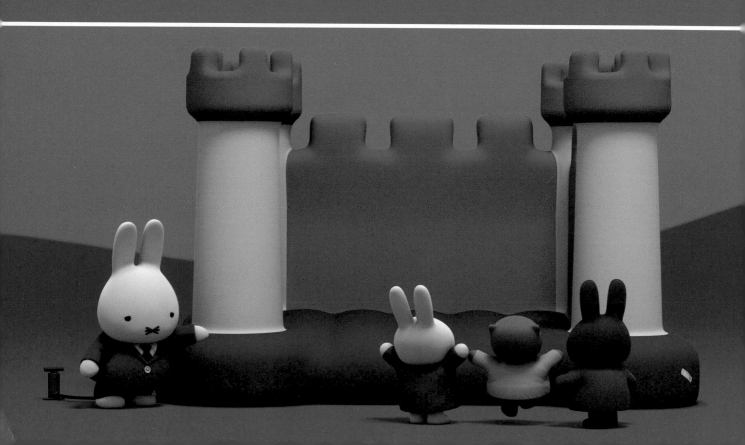